For Michael – J.W.
To Su – T.R.

First published in Great Britain in 2009 by Andersen Press Ltd., 20 Vauxhall Bridge Road, London SW1V 2SA.
Paperback edition first published in 2010 by Andersen Press Ltd.
Published in Australia by Random House Australia Pty., Level 3, 100 Pacific Highway, North Sydney, NSW 2060.

Text copyright © Jeanne Willis, 2009.
Illustration copyright © Tony Ross, 2009.
The rights of Jeanne Willis and Tony Ross to be
identified as the author and illustrator of this work
have been asserted by them in accordance with
the Copyright, Designs and Patents Act, 1988.

10   9   8   7   6   5   4   3   2

British Library Cataloguing in Publication Data available.
ISBN 978 1 84270 925 2(hardback)
ISBN 978 1 84270 945 0 (paperback)
This book has been printed on acid-free paper

BIG BAD BUN

JEANNE WILLIS
and TONY ROSS

Andersen Press

There never was a rabbit as bad as Big Bad Bun –
or so you'd think if you read this letter
which he left on his bed after school one day . . .

Dear Mum and Dad,
I'm sorry to tell you, I HAVE
RUN AWAY FROM HOME. I'm
living at the Dump in Devil's Dyke
with my new best friends.

Home   THE Dump

They call themselves
The Hell Bunnies,
but that is nothing
to what they call
me. They call me
BIG BAD BUN.

I wasn't sure about joining them at first, but they said if I didn't I was a Furry Foo Foo.

So I stayed and now I'm having a lovely time – HONEST!

I passed all the tests they gave me so that I could be a HELL BUNNY too.

Being buried up to my nose in cowpats wasn't half as bad as I thought.

Then I had to blow a raspberry at Mr Fox, which was a bit scary 'cos he can run EVER so fast when he's cross.

The worm burger I had to eat tasted YUCK, but I expect that's because I used to be a vegetarian.

You'd hardly recognise me now, Mum.
I've dyed my tail, I'm into leather
and I've had my ear pierced.

I never wash my whiskers

and I always go to bed really late.

When you get to know them, The Hell Bunnies are really sweet guys,

but you'll not want to know what they did to Farmer Giles . . .

YES, YOU DO! They put bunny poo in his chocopops.

Hee Hee   Hee Hee Hee

And again when I did a wheelie over the pigsty.

I never wear a crash helmet, but I don't give a flying furball.

Sorry to say rude words, but that's how we Hell Bunnies speak.

As I write this, The Weasel Crew have ridden into our camp and started a bun fight . . .

I'VE BEEN HIT!

Don't worry, the red blobs on this page are just jam . . . I HOPE.

I must dash. If you never see me
again, please give my baby sister a
kiss, and try not to blame yourselves.
Your loving son,
BIG BAD BUN (once known as Fluff)

P.S. None of this letter is true. I'm at Grandma's house.

I just wanted to remind you that there are worse things in life

than my TERRIBLE school report.

which is hidden
under my pillow ...

SCHOOL OF FURRY EDUCATION

1 Cabbage Row, Hatch Lane, Hopshire.

HEADMASTER: MR BUCK WARREN

SCHOOL REPORT

FROM: Miss Burrows, Teacher

TO: Mr and Mrs Jumper, Hole 13, Slightly Common, Hopshire

PUPIL: Fluff E Jumper

SUBJECTS

READING: Fluff can read every label in the vegetable garden but his writing will never improve unless he stops gnawing all the pencils.

WRITING: Fluff entertains the class with wild tales but often digs himself into a hole. If he continues to escape under the fence he will not be allowed on our trip to the Rabbit Pellet factory.

ARITHMETIC: Fluff is more interested in rolling about in the clover than learning how to count, yet he knows exactly how many carrots there are in a row. Please remind him not to nibble in class.

PHYSICAL EDUCATION: Fluff is excellent at hopping, skipping and jumping. However he must stop leaping about during assembly.

GENERAL COMMENTS: Fluff is bright-eyed and has a fine pair of ears. Unfortunately he never uses them to listen to his teacher. Unless he wishes to end up in a pie, he must pull his little cotton socks up.

Signed: *Miss Burrows*

P.P.S. You can come and fetch me when you've stopped being cross.

Only PLEASE hurry up, I'm STARVING, and Grandma's cabbage STINKS! Fluff x x x

So at the end of the day, Bun wasn't so big,
and he wasn't so bad –
which just goes to show you can't always
believe everything you read.